WELSH TALES
FOR CHILDREN

Told by Showell Styles

D1511038

JOHN JONES

WELSH TALES FOR CHILDREN

First published May 1989

Cover design by Linda Lovatt (illustration)
and Alison Payne (graphics)

All the illustrations in this book are by final year students, illustration course,
at Wrexham College of Art. The publishers wish to extend
special thanks to Mr Eifion Williams.

ISBN 1 871083 25 7

Printed by Dinefwr Press, Llandybie, Carmarthenshire.

Published by
JOHN JONES PUBLISHING LTD.
Clwydfro Business Centre
Ruthin
North Wales
LL15 1NJ

CONTENTS

Illustrations by:

Owen Glendower's Escape.

Owen Glendower's Escape

This is a true story about a real person, and if you visit Beddgelert you can see where it all happened.

Owen Glendower was a prince of the royal Welsh blood in the time of King Henry the Fourth. In his own country he was called Owain Glyndŵr, but the English lords at the court of King Henry, where Owen was a courtier and soldier, found it easier to say 'Glendower'. These noblemen used to sneer at Owen and call him 'barefoot Welshman', and when one of them, Lord Grey of Ruthin, stole some of Owen's lands the young prince decided that the time had come to fight against his enemies. He went back to Wales, proclaimed himself Prince of Wales by right, and called on all Welsh fighting-men to help him free their country from English rule.

For a time the rebellion succeeded. Owen's men won fight after fight against the men-at-arms which the English lords sent to conquer them. But when King Henry ordered a large army to march into Wales and capture the Prince, the tide of battle turned and the Welsh were defeated. Owen's fighting-men began to desert him and soon he was left quite alone in the mountains of North Wales, with King Henry's soldiers hunting him in every valley.

The Prince had a good friend who lived near Beddgelert, close to the highest mountain in Wales. This was Rhys Goch Eryri — Red Reece of Snowdon — and he was called 'Red' because of his fiery-red hair and beard. Journeying by night, Owen came to Reece's house and knocked cautiously on the door. When his friend saw who it was he welcomed the Prince warmly and told him he should stay as long as he wished.

"Danger brings me here, Reece," said Owen, "and I bring danger with me, for if I am found in your house the King's men will hang you."

"I'll chance that," laughed Red Reece. "One of my fellows shall keep watch up the Colwyn valley, for that's the way Henry's soldiers will come, if they come at all."

So Owen found refuge there, and for a short time his hiding-place was not discovered. Then, one morning, Reece's watchman came racing up to the house to report a large force of the King's men approaching along the Colwyn valley.

"You have been betrayed, my lord Prince," said Reece. "They will surely come to search my house. You and I must take to the mountains and hide.

Owen shook his head. "I am the hunted one, not you," he said. "I go alone."

"I go with you," Red Reece told him firmly. "Quick — put on this old cloak and hat, and I'll dress myself in the same way. If they see us they'll think we're a couple of servants."

Owen did as he said, and they slipped out of the back door onto the hillside just as the soldiers approached the front door and spread out to surround the house. Some leafy thickets gave good cover for Owen and Reece at first and they scrambled up the lower hillside without being seen. But on the bare rocky slope above there was no cover, and a keen-eyed soldier down by the house saw them and reported that two servants were running away from the house.

"Running away!" said the captain of the troop. "Then one of them will be Glendower. After them, men!"

Up the hillside rushed the soldiers like a pack of hounds on the scent. Luckily for the fugitives there was no bowman among them, or they would have been shot down. But the soldiers, armed with swords and daggers, were men picked specially for this sort of chase and they were as fast over steep rough ground as Owen and Reece.

"They'll have us yet," panted Reece as they ran. "You dodge aside when we get behind the rocks yonder — I'll lead them staight on."

The pursuers were hot on their heels and there was no time to argue. Owen ducked out of sight and Reece, with a defiant yell, raced on. The soldiers followed him. And then Reece's hat flew from his head, revealing his fiery-red hair and beard.

"That red fox isn't Glendower!" shouted the captain. "Look — there goes our man!"

Owen was running downhill towards the Pass of Aberglaslyn. In those days the sea came right up to the western end of the Pass, and his plan was to reach it and escape by boat. But the captain of the troop guessed what he was about and sent his fastest runners to cut him off. Owen was forced to swerve back to the right, in the direction of the big mountain called Moel Hebog which stands above Beddgelert. He splashed across the River Glaslyn, thigh-deep in the water, and climbed as fast as he could up the rough hillside. Behind him the pursuing soldiers spread out in a wide crescent to prevent him from escaping to one side or the other. Soon he was high up on Moel Hebog, with the dark cliffs that defend its summit close above him.

Owen had hoped to cross the ridge on the left and escape into Cwm Pennant on the other side. But now he saw the soldiers closing in on that side and knew he could never reach the ridge. He made across to the right — but there too were the clambering figures of King Henry's men. He was being driven up against the foot of the cliffs, and no man had ever found a way to climb them. Owen Glendower was trapped.

If you look up at Moel Hebog from Beddgelert you'll see the cliffs stretching away to the left below the top of the mountain. You may be able to make out the dark line of a cleft in the middle of the cliffs. Owen Glendower saw this cleft just when it seemed certain that he would be captured, and climbed up towards it at top speed. It was as steep and narrow as a chimney and nearly three hundred feet from bottom to top, but it was his only chance and he got into it and began to climb. One slip, and he really would have fallen into the hands of his enemies, probably with a broken neck. But Owen was a fine cragsman and he didn't slip. By the time the breathless soldiers reached the foot of the cleft he was more than halfway to the top.

The captain ordered his troop to follow, but every man refused. They were soldiers, they said, not mountain-goats! The captain decided that he wasn't a mountain-goat either, and they gave up the chase and retreated down the mountainside. As for Owen Glendower, he climbed out at the top of his chimney and made his way to cave in the side of a mountain called Moel yr Ogof (you can see it from the road a mile north of Beddgelert) where he hid himself in safety. Red Reece kept him secretly supplied with food until the soldiers had left the valley, and then Owen came out of hiding to rally his men and fight once more against his enemies.

More than five centuries afterwards, the rock-climbers of our own time have published a guidebook to the climbing 'routes' on Moel Hebog. It describes each climb and records who made the 'first ascent' and when. This is how one of the routes is described:

"Glyndwr's Gully. 250 feet. First Ascent, Owain Glyndwr, circa 1400."

So you see, the story **must** be true.

Collen and the Otherworld King.

Collen and the Otherworld King

In a little stone hut on the hillside there lived a hermit named Collen. He was a big strong man, was Collen, and had been a warrior, but he had decided to exchange his armour for a ragged brown robe and become a holy hermit. He was such a good man that he became a Saint, and when a church was built in the valley it was called Llan Gollen, the Church of Collen, and a town grew up round it.

Collen used to spend a lot of his time in prayer and meditation, and he was meditating one day in his stone cell when he heard two shepherds talking on the hillside close to the cell. They were talking about Gwyn son of Nudd, which was the name given to the King of the Otherworld by Welsh people. The Otherworld is the world of fairies and demons. **Y tylwyth teg**, or The Fair Small Folk, is what the fairies are called in Wales, and they can be cruel and wicked as well as just mischievous.

"I tell you, Tom," one of the shepherds was saying, "Gwyn son of Nudd is king only of the fairies."

"And I tell you," said the other, "that he is king of the demons as well."

"Whichever it is," said the first shepherd, "we ought to find a way to serve him. He would be good friend to have, in this world or the next."

At this Collen, who was listening, was very angry and stuck his head out of the cell door.

"Hold your tongues, ignorant fools!" he told them. "The one you speak of is no better than a devil, as you should know."

His deep voice made the shepherds jump, and they began to walk away scowling.

"You'd better hold your own tongue, Collen," said Tom as they went. "If Gwyn son of Nudd hears what you said of him, you'll be in trouble."

Collen thought there might be some truth in that saying, but he went calmly back to his meditations. It was only a minute or two later that there came a knocking on his cell door. When he called out to ask who was there a smooth voice answered.

"This is the command of Gwyn, King of the Otherworld. You will come and speak with him on the top of the green mound at noon."

"I'll see about it," replied Collen; and he didn't put so much as a toe outside his door for the rest of the day.

Next morning the knocking came again, and the same message. Collen gave exactly the same answer; and he didn't put so much as an eyelash outside his door that day.

On the morning of the third day the unseen messenger knocked again, and this time his voice was not so smooth.

"King Gwyn wishes to be your friend, but if you will not come to the top of the green mound at noon he will send his warriors to carry you there."

"I'll see about it," said Collen; but what he **did** see was that he would have to obey, if only to put an end to this nuisance.

So he put a big flask full of holy water in the pocket of his robe and climbed up to the top of the green mound at noon. Great was his wonder when he found there a splendid castle surrounded by beautiful gardens and meadows, with knights in shining armour galloping merrily in the meadows and handsome youths dancing with lovely maidens in the gardens. Music sounded on every hand from bands of minstrels with harps and sweet-voiced horns. And all these people were young and gay except a tall man in glittering robes who stood on the castle wall. This man had a jewelled crown on his head, and was so grave and noble of bearing that Collen, against his will, had to show respect for him.

"Lord," he said, "the greeting that is your right be with you."

"My greeting to you, Collen," replied the King, "and the greeting of my two kingdoms with it. Be pleased to enter my castle and speak with me."

Collen went in through the great doorway and the richly-dressed youths and maidens went in behind him. He found a golden table set in the midst of a splendid hall, with a throng of squires dressed in red and blue waiting to serve the tempting foods and drinks. King Gwyn was sitting in a golden chair at the other end of the table.

"Be seated, Collen," he said kindly, "and if you see nothing here to please you, tell me your desire and you shall have it, whatever it may be. If you are hungry — why, sit down with me and eat and drink."

But Collen did not sit down. "I will not eat the leaves of trees nor drink the dew from the grass," said he. "And I think you understand me, King Gwyn."

The King frowned, but changed it to a smile. "You have understood **me**, Collen," he said. "I wish you to stay with me and be my counsellor. Every honour shall be yours and your smallest wish shall be granted, if you will wear my colours of red and blue. Do not my squires look fine in their tunics? Your robes shall be of finest red and blue silks."

"I would not wear those colours for all the wealth of the world," said Collen boldly.

The King stood up, and now he was frowning blackly indeed.

"Why not?" he demanded.

"Because red means burning and blue means freezing," replied Collen. "And now you understand me well, King Gwyn."

With that, he took the flask of holy water from his pocket, pulled out the stopper, and scattered the water over all that stood round him. Instantly the castle and the folk in it vanished into the air. There were no gardens and meadows, no men and maidens, no galloping knights and no sweet-voiced music. There was just the grassy mound on the hillside with the sun shining on it.

Collen liked it better that way. He went gladly down to his cell, where he was never again disturbed by the knocking of King Gwyn's messengers. And he put his toes, and his eyelashes, outside the cell door just whenever he liked.

A Fairy Marriage.

A Fairy Marriage

About five miles north of Beddgelert, at the highest point of the road that crosses the pass into Nantlle, is a lake called Llyn-y-Dywarchen. The name means in English 'Lake of the Turf,' and it was so called because there was an island of turf in the lake. No ordinary island was this, for it floated about like a raft and was sometimes touching the shore and sometimes out in the middle of the lake. It was still there two hundred years ago, but now it has gone — removed by the Fair Small Folk, no doubt, so that what happened in this story could not happen again.

It happened that the son of the farm called Drws-y-Coed, which is in the valley below the lake, was minding the sheep on the mountain-side one misty day. One or two of the sheep strayed towards the lake, so the young man ran across the moorland to fetch them back. There was no island in the lake then, but he saw something much more interesting — a most beautiful girl standing on the lake shore all dripping wet, as if she had just come up out of the water. This is how he described her when he told the story long afterwards: "Her golden hair hung in curled locks, her eyes were of the blue of the clear sky, and on each round cheek was a red rose." He went towards her and asked if he might speak with her and be her friend, and at once she held out her hand to him with a smile and said: "Man of all my dreams, you have come at last."

This was all that was needed to make the young man fall madly in love with her. When they had finished their talk, the lovely girl walked into the lake and vanished below its shining waters, which showed him plainly that she was one of the Fair Small Folk. But even that could not make the young man love her any the less. Indeed, his love gave him no peace, day or night, and though after that first time they often met by the lake shore he could not bear to see her leave him and always begged her, at parting, to marry him so that they could be together always.

At last the fairy girl said she would marry him, but only if her father gave his consent. The young man must wait in the trees by the lake, she said, until the moon had gone down behind the mountain called Y Garn, and at that time she would bring her father to meet him. So he waited there until the moon went down, and as soon as the shadow of Y Garn fell across the trees the fairy girl appeared with her father, who could not be well seen because of the darkness.

"You shall have my daughter," said the father straight away, "and with her this bag of gold for her dowry, but on one condition. You must never allow her to be touched with iron. If ever **that thing** touches her, she will return to her own people and never come to you on the soil of this earth again."

The young man was not surprised, for he had heard that the Fair Small Folk hated iron so much that they disliked even the name of it. He gladly consented to the condition. The fairy father vanished, the fairy girl put her hand into her husband's hand, and the happy pair went home to the farm taking the bag of gold with them.

For a number of years the young man and his fairy wife lived contentedly together and had several children. The fairy gold made them rich and prosperous, so that the mountain shepherd became the owner of many farms and flocks of sheep and fine horses. He took great care that nothing made of iron should ever touch his wife, and saw to it that no iron was used on the saddle and bridle and stirrups of her horse. For often they would ride together to market, or to visit friends. It was when they were riding back from a visit to Beddgelert that the fatal thing happened.

In those days there was no road up the Colwyn valley, only a rough track, and this ran close by the marshy shore of Llyn-y-Gadair. The horse of the fairy girl slipped from the track into the marsh, and in a moment sank to the saddle-girths. The man sprang down and managed to pull both out safely, but the girl was so frightened that she would not ride her horse again.

"Then you must ride pillion behind me," said the husband, "and we will lead your horse."

He got into the saddle and reached a hand to help her up behind him. And in so doing her knee touched the metal of his stirrup-iron.

For a short time nothing happened. They rode on up the hillside towards the pass of Drws-y-Coed, she with her arms clasped round his waist as she sat behind him, and the led horse following. Then, by ones and twos, small figures clothed in green began to be seen on the hillside, appearing and disappearing among the rocks. Also a strange sweet music sounded distantly, as if it came from inside the hill. Quite suddenly the husband found that there were no longer two soft arms clasping his waist, and no beloved wife sitting behind him. The music ceased, the small green figures vanished — and the fairy wife was gone.

Great indeed was the grief of the husband, for he knew well that what the fairy father had told him had now come true. She would never come to him on the soil of this earth again. He went sadly home, to tell his children of their loss and comfort them as best he could. But though he could not guess it, there was to be a happy ending to his sorrowful tale.

In the Otherworld beneath the lake waters the fairy wife was pleading with her mother,and between them they found a way to overcome the fairy ban. So it came about that one day, when the sad husband was minding his sheep near the shores of Llyn-y-Dywarchen, he saw to his amazement that there was an island in the lake, and that this island was moving towards the shore in a manner that showed it was not the soil of this earth. Not only that, but there on the island stood his fairy wife, stretching out her arms to him.

The joy of their meeting can be imagined. And afterwards they met as often as they liked on the floating island and spent many happy hours there, so that in spite of all that had happened the farmer of Drws-y-Coed lived happily until the last day of his life.

The Giant who Collected Beards.

16

The Giant who Collected Beards

You'd have a job to find two kings more silly and vain than Nyniaw and Peibiaw, who were kings in Wales a long time ago. They boasted and bragged whenever they met to wag beards together, and one king couldn't claim to have something without the other king claiming to have the same thing only better.

"Look at my wide pasture-field, King Peibiaw," said Nyniaw one day. "It's the finest in the whole world. You've got no pasture as wide as that, my friend!"

"Oh yes I have, King Nyniaw," said Peibiaw. "In fact, it's a thousand times wider than yours, so there!"

"Ha, ha," said Nyniaw nastily. "I'll believe that when I see it."

"All right then!" said Peibiaw. "Be here in this place tonight and I'll show it to you."

Nyniaw was too inquisitive to miss that appointment so the two of them met at the same place when the night sky was cloudless and full of stars.

"Now!" said Peibiaw. "Just look at my splendid pasture and tell me if your miserable fields can compare with it."

"Where is it?" asked Nyniaw, staring all round him.

Peibiaw pointed overhead. "There!" he said. "The whole of the sky is my pasture. Deny that if you dare!"

"Oh, I don't deny it," returned Nyniaw with a chuckle. "It's a good pasture, that. I'm glad to see my flocks and herds grazing all over it."

"Eh?" exclaimed Peibiaw, peering angrily into the sky. "Where are they?"

"Those things that look like stars are my cows and sheep," said Nyniaw. "Thousands of them, aren't there?"

17

"**Esgob mawr!**" Peibiaw shouted. "Get them out of there this minute, or I'll send my army to drive them out."

"Oh, you will, will you?" said Nyniaw, getting angry. "And what will my army be doing, meanwhile?"

"Running away," roared Peibiaw. "That's all they ever do."

"Send your miserable army and see what happens!" yelled Nyniaw.

"And I'll do just that!" bellowed Peibiaw.

Then the two kings turned their backs on each other and hurried away to get their armies ready for battle.

Now Rhitta the Giant was the chief king of North Wales at this time, and he lived on Snowdon and lorded it over the twenty-eight lesser kings of the country. When he heard of the quarrel between Nyniaw and Peibiaw he was very shocked indeed.

"**Esgob mawr!**" he said in his great booming voice. "What fools these kings are! Don't they know that I own the pasture in the skies? I must teach them a lesson."

And he gathered a great army and came storming down the mountainsides just as the smaller armies of Nyniaw and Peibiaw met in battle. The two kings had no chance against Rhitta's army and they were captured at once. Rhitta had them brought before him, gave them a severe lecture, and punished them by cutting off their beards. The punishment was the greatest insult Rhitta could think of, for he himself was proud of his splendid beard, which was large and thick, black in colour but speckled with white. Indeed, when people look out of the door and see a dark night with the snow falling, they say: "Dear me! It's as thick as Rhitta's beard."

To make the insult worse, Rhitta had the two beards made into a cap.

"I shall wear this," he told Nyniaw and Peibiaw, "when I go night-walking in the fields to count my sheep in the sky."

It really served the two kings right for being so silly. But the other twenty-six kings in Wales didn't like Rhitta's behaviour at all, especially as they all had beards and were proud of them. They decided to take their armies to Snowdon and teach the Giant that he must show more respect for royalties with hair on their chins.

"He must learn," they said, "that in insulting Nyniaw and Peibiaw by cutting off their beards he has insulted each one of us in the same way."

"That," said Rhitta when he heard of this, "is a very good idea."

And he charged down the mountainside just as the twenty-six kings were getting ready to attack him and captured them, every man. Then he removed the beards from the kings' chins and had them stitched into a cape.

"I shall wear this round my shoulders," he told them, "when I go night-walking in the fields to count my sheep in the sky."

The twenty-six kings went sadly home rubbing their cold chins and grumbling. They grumbled so much that the news of what had happened soon spread to all the other kings of Britain, and they too gathered their armies and marched to punish Rhitta for insulting their fellow-kings.

"If this sort of thing goes on," they said, "there won't be a single beard left in Britain."

But their armies and their marching did no good, because Rhitta met them in battle and defeated them utterly. He captured all the kings — there were dozens and dozens of them — and cut off all their beards. There were nearly enough to make his cape into a fine cloak, just the thing for a night-walking and counting sheep in the sky, but the cloak had a large gap in it which only a fine big beard could fill. By now Rhitta the Giant had become a keen collector of king's beards and was determined to fill that gap in his cloak. So when he heard of a new king far down in the south, a king who had a splendid golden beard, he sent off a messenger at once demanding his beard, which would be exactly the right colour to finish off the pattern of the cloak of beards.

The new king in the south was none other than King Arthur. The answer he sent back to Rhitta was quite polite. It said that King Arthur's beard wasn't ready for use in a giant's cloak just yet, but if Rhitta liked to come south with his army an even more suitable beard would be found for him. So Rhitta put on his almost-finished cloak of beards and marched southward with all his army, resolving to have Arthur's beard and not to take any substitute. As they came near the place where Arthur awaited him there was a flashing like lightning in the southern sky and a great roaring like thunder.

"What may that be?" asked the Giant, halting in dismay.

"Lord," they said, "the flashing is the bright armour of Arthur's knights, and the roaring is the cheer with which they greet him."

At this Rhitta trembled. And he trembled still more when his army came in sight of Arthur's army, for the tread of the great king's men shook the earth and their numbers were more than the stars that Rhitta pretended were his sheep.

"What plan of battle must we use?" he asked his leaders.

"Only one plan," they replied. "We must yield, and quickly."

And all Rhitta's men dropped their swords and shields on the ground. The Giant saw that he would have to give in, so he made the best he could of it. He pulled his cloak of beards round him and went forward to meet Arthur in the space between the two armies.

"Well, Giant Rhitta," King Arthur greeted him. "Do you still want to have my beard?"

"No," growled Rhitta. "But you said you'd find me another one. Where is it?".

"On your chin, Rhitta," said Arthur, and at his words a great shout of laughter went up from his army.

The Giant went down on his knees to beg for mercy, for he was very fond indeed of his fine beard, but though Arthur was a merciful king he was also a just one, and he thought it was about time Rhitta's beard-collecting came to an end.

"Off with his beard!" he ordered, and Cadw of Pictland stepped forward with a flaying-knife and flayed off that fine black beard speckled with white.

'I see the gap in your cloak is at the very bottom of the hem," Arthur went on. "That's a very good place for your beard, Rhitta. You shall sew it on there, and you shall wear the cloak for the rest of your life."

At this Rhitta began to protest, but King Arthur cut him short.

"Who is your overlord, Giant?" he demanded sternly.

"You are, King Arthur," muttered Rhitta. "And I'll do as you say."

So he stitched his own beard to the cloak of beards and went back again to Snowdon. And he wore the cloak to the end of his days, as a badge of his servitude.

A Land Under the Sea.

A Land Under the Sea

A long time ago, before people began writing history-books, there was a fine rich countryside in the west of North Wales. You can't visit it now, because where it used to be there is only the big blue plain of the sea in Cardigan Bay. But if you look seaward from the hills behind Barmouth on a clear day, when the tide's low and the sea is calm, you'll see a line of white foam far out on the blue surface, where the waves are breaking on the ruin of the wall that used to keep the sea from flooding that fine rich countryside.

The land of Gwaelod, it was called, and it was all below sea-level. It had twenty towns in it, and churches and roads and fields of wheat and barley, and they say the busiest ports of Britain were on its shore. The people of Gwaelod went about their business without a care in the world, although at the high tides the sea outside their land was well above the level of their heads. Hadn't they a great strong sea-wall all along the western coast to keep the sea out? And hadn't the king appointed two princes to look after the wall? They thought themselves quite safe in Gwaelod with Prince Teithrin and Prince Seithenin watching over their defences.

Prince Seithenin had charge of the south part of the sea-wall, which joined with the higher land close to where Aberdovey is now. If you know where Shell Island is, you know where the north end of the wall was. It came to Mochras Point, between Barmouth and Harlech, which many people call Shell Island nowadays. Prince Teithrin had the north part of the wall in his care, and he was a very good sort of young man as princes go, taking his duties seriously and seeing to it that his half of the sea-wall was always in good repair. Seithenin was quite the opposite. He was older than Teithrin and had a beautiful daughter named Rhonwen, but he was a terrible drunkard. He had built a fine castle right on the sea-wall, and used to boast that he kept watch on his enemy the sea without having to leave his castle, but what he really did was to spend all his time having drinking-parties with his friends in the castle hall, while the repairing of the wall was left to his servants. 'Like master, like man,' says the proverb.

Seithenin's servants were just as drunken and careless as their master, so the south part of the sea-wall got more and more broken by the waves until parts of it were almost ready to collapse.

Teithrin had a good idea of what was going on. But being a modest lad he didn't like to reproach the older prince with his folly. Besides, Seithenin was Rhonwen's father, and the young man hoped one day to ask him for his daughter's hand in marriage. By the time he had made up his mind that Seithenin **must** be asked to have those weak places in the wall repaired, it was too late. There blew up out of the west a tremendous storm, at the very time of the highest tide of the year, and Teithrin and his men hurried along the northern wall making a close inspection of its defences. All was well there, but the prince found himself very worried about the wall farther south where the weak places were — especially as Rhonwen lived in her father's castle there.

Telling his men to keep watch on the rising waves, he went as fast as he could along the causeway on top of the wall towards Seithenin's castle.

As he went the storm grew fiercer and the waves dashed higher and higher over the sea-wall. The day was darkening towards night, but even in the dim light Teithrin could see the cracks in the stonework, and at one place he saw a great sea smash a hole in the masonry. Each giant blow as a wave broke against the barrier set the wall shuddering and shaking under his feet. At this rate, thought Teithrin, it won't be long before the wall gives way, and Seithenin's castle will fall with it. And he began to run.

Dodging through the cascades of spray, he reached the castle door at last and rushed through it into the great hall. The whole castle was trembling under the shocks of wave and wind, but nobody in the hall was worrying about that. Seithenin's companions lay on the floor in a drunken stupor, and Prince Seithenin himself was sitting at the table with a huge wine-cup at his lips.

"Rouse your servants instantly, Seithenin!" Teithrin cried to him. "They must bring stone and mend the wall."

Seithenin put down the wine-cup and blinked at him.

"Why, it's young Teithrin," he said in a thick voice. "Sit down and have a drink, young Teithrin. Servants? They're all fast asleep, bless 'em."

Teithrin saw there was nothing to be done with the drunken prince. He raised his own voice, shouting for men to come and help him. No one replied. He dashed outside the castle again, shouting as he ran, but no one came. And he was in time to see an enormous wave batter down the top of the sea-wall and the dark water come pouring in through the gap. Then someone clutched his arm. It was Seithenin's daughter Rhonwen.

"The castle will fall!" she cried above the uproar of the storm. "Teithrin — you must save my father!"

The young prince turned and ran back into the castle hall with Rhonwen at his heels. Seithenin was still sitting in drunken contentment with the wine-cup in his hand.

"Come out, Seithenin!" Teithrin yelled at him. "The wall is breached and your enemy is through the breach!"

He had roused the drunkard now. Seithenin tossed the wine-cup aside and rose unsteadily.

"Enemy?" he repeated, drawing his sword. "Show me the enemy that can stand against Seithenin!"

Before they could stop him he had rushed past Teithrin and Rhonwen, out onto the sea-wall. A tremendous wave knocked him flat, but he staggered to his feet as the two ran out after him.

"A treacherous blow!" he shouted. "Have at ye, traitors!"

Then, sword in hand and bawling his warcry, he leapt from the wall straight into the advancing waves.

Teithrin caught Rhonwen in his arms, for she had seen her father's fate and was nearly fainting. But a loud crack and a roar like thunder made him look up — to see the main tower of the castle crumble and fall into the raging sea. The way northward along the wall was blocked by the sea that poured through the breach and there was only one way of escape left to them. Teithrin grasped Rhonwen's hand and they began to climb across the fallen stonework of the tower, with the huge waves leaping up from below and trying to drag them down.

How long it was before they at last reached the hillsides above the wall, or how long they lay under a thicket of hazels in a sleep of exhaustion, neither of them knew. But when they woke it was morning, and the storm had passed. Teithrin and Rhonwen went hand-in-hand to the summit of a hill nearby, from which they could look out and see how much damage had been done to the unhappy land of Gwaelod. But of the twenty towns, and the churches and roads, and the fields of wheat and barley, nothing at all was to be seen. The land of Gwaelod had vanished for ever. Where it had been was only the big blue plain of the sea in Cardigan Bay.

The Story of Gelert

This is a sad story. A good one to read after it would be The Golden Harp, **or** Mule's Ears.

In the time of Prince Llewelyn the valleys below Snowdon were thickly clothed with forests, and the forests were full of wild animals. Foxes and wolves as well as stags and hares roamed there, and except for a hunting-lodge in a forest clearing, where the River Colwyn meets the River Glaslyn, there was no town or village for miles around.

Prince Llewelyn was very fond of hunting. He came to stay at the hunting-lodge with his servants and horses and hounds, and with him came his wife Princess Joan and their baby son. There was a nurse to look after the baby, so that the Princess could go out hunting with her husband. One day they all set off into the forest to hunt the stag, the Prince and Princess on their horses, the servants on foot, and the hounds trotting beside them eager for the chase. Only the nurse was left behind, to look after the baby who was asleep in his cradle. And no sooner had the hunting-party gone than the man who was courting the nurse came to the house and took her off for a walk in the woods. The door of the house was left open.

Meanwhile the hounds had picked up the trail of a stag. They were big dogs, faithful and brave, and the bravest and most faithful of all was Gelert. Llewelyn was very fond of Gelert, who never failed to be first on the scent and boldest in attacking the quarry. When the Prince noticed that today Gelert was not among the other hounds he reined-in his horse at once, and asked if anyone had seen the dog.

"Gelert was with us until we crossed that last stream, my lord," said one of the servants.

"I saw him going back by the way we came," said another.

Princess Joan touched her husband's arm. "Gelert must have gone back to the house," she said anxiously. "Can something be wrong there?"

The Story of Gelert.

At this Llewellyn was worried too. He gave the order to abandon the hunt, and they began to go back through the forest, the Prince and Princess cantering ahead on their horses. As they came in sight of the house they saw Gelert come out and run towards them, wagging his tail. But when he came closer the Princess gave a cry and sank fainting from her horse, for the dog was all smeared and dripping with blood.

Leving his wife to the care of the servants, Llewelyn galloped to the house, flung himself from the saddle, and rushed inside. A terrible sight met his eyes. Pools of blood lay on the floor of the room where the baby had been left. Blood stained the torn tapestries that were scattered everywhere and the pile of bed-clothes beside the overturned cradle. And the cradle itself was empty.

Llewelyn's grief and horror turned to wild anger. It was plain that his only child had been dragged from the cradle and killed. He turned and saw Gelert — Gelert with blood dripping from his jaws. There was the culprit! In a frenzy of rage he drew his sword and plunged it deep into the dog's side, and with one last yelp poor Gelert sank down, dead.

Then, like an echo of that dying cry, there came a smaller cry from beneath the pile of bedclothes. Llewelyn dragged them aside, and saw his baby lying there safe and unhurt. Next moment one of his servants gave a loud exclamation. The man had raised a bloodstained tapestry from the floor, revealing beneath it the dead body of an enormous grey wolf, slain by brave Gelert in defence of the child.

With tears streaming down his cheeks, the Prince fell on his knees beside the dead hound. Too late he saw that the dog's instinct had told him the baby was in danger, and that Gelert had been just in time to save his son's life. At last he stood up, his heart heavy with sorrow for what he had done, and gave orders to those round him.

"Take Gelert's body to the green meadow called Dol-y-Lleian," he said, "and bury him there with all the honour due to a hero. Raise a great stone above his grave. All who pass this way shall be shown it and told the story of faithful Gelert, and of the master who in his cruel haste slew his best friend."

This was done. In after years a village was built at that place and called Bedd Gelert, the Grave of Gelert. And to this very day you can see the grave in the field close to the village, with a stone slab by it inscribed with the Story of Gelert.

The Golden Harp.

The Golden Harp

A merry couple were Morgan Preece and his wife Anna. You wouldn't find a merrier in the whole of Wales. They lived in a little white cottage on the lane that runs up from Dolgellau onto the flanks of Cader Idris, and the jokes and the laughing they had together would have done your heart good to hear. Morgan made Anna laugh most when he tried to sing, or to play on Anna's harp, for he had a voice like a crow and his thick fingers were too clumsy to pluck the harp-strings. He didn't mind being made fun of by Anna, for he was a kind-hearted man and loved his wife very much. But he wasn't so pleased by the sneers of his neighbour Evan Jones, who had a fine tenor voice himself and lived a little way down the lane.

One evening Morgan was sitting by his fire waiting for Anna to come back from Dolgellau, where she had gone to sing at a **noson lawen**. Knock, knock, knock there was on the door, and when he opened it there stood three small men in green cloaks.

"Sir," said the smallest of them, "we have journeyed far and are very tired. If you would be kind enough to give us a little food and drink we could go on our way more easily."

"Come in, come in!" said Morgan heartily. "I've little enough in the house until my wife comes back from Dolgellau, but what there is you may have and welcome. Will bread and cheese and a mug of ale suit you?"

As he spoke he was bustling about his little parlour, seating his guests at the table, opening cupboards and peering into them.

"Why, here's one of Anna's cakes, too," he said bringing it to the travellers. "No one bakes such good cakes as Anna. Eat and drink as much as you want, my friends, for no one goes away empty from the house of Morgan Preece."

The three travellers ate and drank in silence, which Morgan thought a little strange. When they had finished they stood up, and the smallest man spoke.

31

"You have shown us much kindness, Morgan Preece," he said, "and we would like to repay it. Ask for whatever you want and we will give it you."

Morgan felt pretty sure they were joking with him, so he spoke jokingly in reply.

"Well, then," he said with a chuckle, "Anna keeps telling me I'll never play the harp with my clumsy fingers, and I'm afraid she's just about right. What I'd like is a harp that I **can** play."

"Very well," said the smallest man at once. "There it is."

He pointed to the fireplace, and when Morgan looked he saw standing on the hearthrug the most beautiful little harp that ever was made. It was of shining gold set with jewels that sparkled red and green in the firelight.

"**Bobol anwyl!**" he exclaimed. "Where did that come from?"

But there was no reply from the three travellers. They had vanished. Then Morgan knew that he had been entertaining three of the Fairy Folk who lived in the rocks of Cader Idris, and he was a little bit frightened. Still, there was the golden harp waiting to be played, so he took it up cautiously and placed his clumsy fingers on the strings. Sure enough, the harp began to play, and without Morgan's help! It played all the lively Welsh dance-tunes he knew, and more beside, and it was still playing when Anna came home.

The moment she came in through the door, before even she could give Morgan a kiss, Anna began to dance. She danced round the table, and in and out of the house, and round the chairs, until she was exhausted.

"Stop! Stop!" she cried breathlessly as she danced.

"Well, then, **you** stop if you want to," said Morgan.

"I **can't** stop!" Anna panted.

So Morgan put the harp down and at once it stopped playing and Anna flopped into a chair. As soon as she had her breath back she began to laugh, and Morgan too, and when they'd done laughing he told her how he had come by the harp.

That was only the beginning of it, for the news soon spread and the people from the cottages round all came in, night after night, to see the golden harp and dance to its music. Sometimes Morgan would have some fun by keeping them dancing when they wanted to stop, but he never went on long enough to make them angry or tired. There was just the one time when he did that.

It was when Anna was away at Dolgellau market one day. Evan Jones knocked at the door and put his head in.

"I've just looked in, Mr Preece," he said nastily, "to say I don't believe what they're saying. I know you haven't a note of music in you so I know you can't play the harp. Good day."

"Just a minute, Mr Jones," said Morgan as he was going.

And he picked up the harp, which was beside him, and began to play. Well, you'd have laughed to see Evan Jones then! He danced and he danced, with his face red and angry, and the bad names he threw at Morgan lasted him until he had no more breath to call names. Morgan went on playing, and Evan Jones went on dancing, until Evan's red face became white and his tired legs began to bend under him and at last he fell down on the doorstep. You wouldn't have laughed then.

"That'll teach you, Evan Jones!" said Morgan, putting the harp down at last.

He shut the door on him, and went to the window to watch him drag himself away down the hill. In his ear then there came a low sweet voice.

"Fairy music was not meant to be played in spite," it said.

Morgan jumped round, but there was nobody there. The golden harp wasn't there, either. It had vanished.

When Anna came back Morgan told her what had happened. "And it was my own fault, Anna," he ended sadly.

"That's very true," she said, shaking her head at him. "But never mind — if you can't play, I can still sing."

And she sang so merrily and sweetly for him that Morgan's sadness vanished as completely as the golden harp had done.

After that they lived happily to the end of their days, and were never spiteful to anyone, not even to Evan Jones. But never again did the fairies bring a gift to Morgan Preece.

The Cave of Knights.

The Cave of Knights

There are two stories here, and the old folk of Beddgelert will tell you that the first one, at any rate, is true.

Not so very long ago, about the year 1850, the shepherd of Hafod-y-Llan farm was gathering the sheep from the high valley of Cwm Tregalan, which is under the ridge between Snowdon and Lliwedd. One of the sheep ran away from the flock and up the mountainside, and he saw it reach the crest of the ridge and disappear over it. Leaving his dogs to keep the flock together, the shepherd climbed to the ridge, and seeing no sign of the sheep decided to climb out along the cliff-face of Lliwedd to look for it. Lliwedd is a precipice, but its many ledges have grass and juicy plants growing on them, so that sheep are sometimes tempted onto these dangerous places.

The shepherd clambered from one ledge to another without finding the sheep, and soon he found himself too high and far out on the cliff for comfort. Just a look round the next corner, he told himself, and then I'll go back. He climbed cautiously round the corner of steep rock, and to his amazement saw the mouth of a deep cave before him. He stepped inside, peering into the darkness. Surely there were men lying in rows on the floor of the cave — or were they pieces of rock? He took another step forward for a closer look, and his shoulder struck against something that hung from the rock-wall above him. It was a great bell, and at the deafening **clang!** it gave forth the shadowy figures started to their feet with a clanking like iron striking iron.

The frightened shepherd did not wait to see more. No mountain goat could have climbed back across the ledges more quickly than he did, and when he reached the mountainside he ran down it as if the Devil was behind him. Pausing only to get his sheep into a fold and send the dogs back to Hafod-y-Llan, he went running down into Nant Gwynant and into Beddgelert village, and stopped only when he was sitting in the inn with a mugful of ale cooling his dry throat. Of course, the men who were there wanted to know what made him run so hard and look so scared. But when he told them they only laughed and accused him of telling lies. Then a very old man who was sitting in the chimney-corner spoke up.

"I believe him," he said, "because I know what men they were that he saw in the cave. I had the story from my grandfather, who had it from **his** grandfather, and so back to my ancestor who was descended from Emrys the Magician."

"All right, **taid**," they said. "Let's have the story."

You must know (began the old man) that King Arthur had driven the pagan Saxons out of North Wales after twelve great battles. It was Medrod, a traitor knight who had once been a knight of the Round Table, who made a treaty with the Saxons and led them back across the moutains into Cwm Tregalan, where they gathered a great army secretly to fall on Arthur and crush him. The great king heard of that treachery. Old though he was, and with all but a few of his knights scattered and dead, he collected such fighting-men as he could get and marched north from his city of Caerleon. They had their camp not two miles from this very inn, in a field below Dinas Emrys. There a shepherd came to King Arthur and told him how Medrod and the Saxon army were hidden in the great cwm of Tregalan, under the brow of Snowdon. Arthur was glad when he heard that. The enemy outnumbered his men by three to one, but at least they could not escape him, for — as you all know — a man may climb out of Cwm Tregalan to the ridge, but on the other side of the ridge is a precipice.

So next day Arthur's army marched into Cwm-y-Llan and up that valley to Cwm Tregalan above it, and there he fought the last battle of his life against the pagans. All day until nightfall it raged, and by then the mountainside was covered with dead men and dying. Arthur rallied the few warriors he had left and drove the remaining Saxons right up to the ridge, where most of them were forced over the precipice to their death. But before their end they loosed a flight of arrows, by one of which the King was wounded to the death. Now, friends, you know why that ridge is called Bwlch-y-Saethau, the Pass of the Arrows.

Arthur pulled the fatal arrow from his side. And as he did so who should come towards him but the traitor Medrod, with his sword upraised to strike. Arthur glanced that blow aside and by a great effort swung up his sword Excalibur. Down came the good blade and cleft through the traitor's helm, stretching him dead among the rocks.

Then it was (some say) that the faithful Bedivere carried the dying King down the precipice to a lake, where he was taken away in a barge to the Isle of Avalon. But those that were left of Arthur's knights, many of them sorely wounded, went into a cave thereabouts to lie down and rest. And there they lie to this day, waiting for the ringing of the bell that will tell them that Arthur has come again and they must awake and fight for him.

"And that," ended the old man, looking round him, "is why I believe the story told by this shepherd. I know, now, that the old tale is true. Would anyone like to say I am telling lies?"

But no one there liked to say that.

You Musn't see the Fairies.

You Musn't see the Fairies

There was an old farmer and his wife of Garth Dorwen, near Caernarvon, who wanted a maidservant. So they went to the All-Hallows fair at Caernarvon, where it was the custom for servants who wanted to be hired to stand in a certain place, and there they saw a beautiful girl with golden hair standing with the others. The old lady was very taken with her, and offered her good wages to take service at Garth Dorwen. The girl accepted and they all three went back to the farm together.

Now the girl, whose name was Eilian, made herself very useful and they were pleased with her, except in one respect. It was winter, and as usual the women of the house sat round the fire spinning, but though Eilian spun as much wool as she should she would only do it outside in the moonlight. This puzzled the farmer and his wife, for it was warm by the fireside and cold out in the moonlight, and one night they hid themselves behind a rock to watch Eilian. The girl sat on a rock spinning her wool for a minute or two, and then she suddenly got up and began to dance in the moonlight, smiling and sometimes laughing. The two watchers crept back to the house, and when Eilian came in and they could get her to themselves they asked what made her go dancing in the moonlight by herself.

"But I don't dance by myself," said the girl. "As soon as they come, I dance with the **tylwyth teg**."

"We saw no fairies!" exclaimed the old dame.

"Of course not, mistress," said Eilian, "and I'm glad you didn't. You mustn't see the fairies unless they want you to see them. If you do, they will be angry."

With that the farmer and his wife had to be satisfied. But it was only a week or two later that Eilian went out to spin in the moonlight and never came back. The fairies had taken her away.

The dame of Garth Dorwen was sorry to lose her, but she was a busy old lady with not much time for worrying about missing servant-girls. For one thing, she was an excellent midwife, and when any wife round about was expecting the arrival of the baby the husband always sent for help at the birth. She wasn't surprised, then, when one misty night a finely-dressed gentleman rode up to the house to fetch her to his wife, whose baby was soon to be born. She got up behind him on his horse, and they rode up the hillside, and into a cave, of all places. Inside the cave was a splendid chamber all richly decorated, with a great fire blazing on the hearth and fine linen ready for the baby when it should come. A beautiful woman was lying in a bed fit for a princess, and the old lady could see that it wouldn't be long before the baby came.

Well, she performed her duties with success, and washed and dressed the new baby. Then the husband brought her a bottle of ointment.

"You must put some of this on the baby's eyes," he told her. "But be very, very careful not to get any of it on your own eyes."

She did as he said, and afterwards put the bottle on a shelf. Just then her left eye began to itch, so she rubbed it with a finger, not realising that a little of the ointment was on that finger. No sooner had she touched her eye than — lo and behold! — she saw with that eye a dark and wretched cavern with no furniture except big stones. A miserable fire was glimmering in a corner and the poor wife, who was none other than her maidservant Eilian, was lying on a bundle of bracken. With the other eye she still saw the splendid chamber and bed fit for a princess.

Next morning the old dame found herself standing on the open hillside, and when she looked for the cave it had vanished. Grumbling a good deal to herself, she made her way back to Garth Dorwen, and glad she was to get there. She was glad, too, to find that she saw just the same things with the one eye as she did with the other. But she hadn't finished yet with the **tylwyth teg**.

It happened that the old dame went one day to Caernarvon market, and there among the crowd she saw the gentleman who had come to fetch her to Eilian's baby. Finely-dressed though he was, none of the people looked at him as he passed them, which seemed rather queer to her. All the same, she went up to him and asked after Eilian and the baby.

"Oh, they're very well," he said, looking at her strangely. "May I ask which eye you see me with?"

"This one," she said, pointing to it.

In a twinkling he pulled a bulrush from his pocket.

"You mustn't see the fairies, dame," he said, and touched her eye with the bulrush.

At once he vanished from her sight, and the old dame of Garth Dorwen never saw another fairy as long as she lived.

Mule's Ears.

Mule's Ears

King March of Lleyn had a secret. This secret made him very sad, and he never smiled at all, though he was the richest king in North Wales and had bags and bags full of gold. He was a good king and ruled wisely, so that the people of Lleyn respected him. But March was quite sure that if they knew his secret they wouldn't respect him any more.

There was one thing about King March that everyone could see. He had never had a haircut. His hair grew so long that he could sit on it, and naturally enough some of his younger subjects used to make jokes about it. March was upset when he heard this, for his secret had made him a very sensitive man. He decided that he must have his hair cut, as far as his shoulders at any rate, even though it meant that one other person beside himself would know his dreadful secret. He sent for a fat little man named Bifan and appointed him court barber, at a very large salary.

"Now, Bifan," said the King when the barber presented himself with scissors and comb, "in cutting my hair you will discover a terrible thing about me. If you speak one word about it to anyone I swear I will cut off your head."

This made Bifan's hand shake with fear as he began to cut the King's long hair, but he managed as best he could. He was terrified of what he might discover, but when he lifted the long hair to trim it, and saw what was underneath, he felt more inclined to laugh. For King March had very long ears, just like mule's ears. Bifan kept his face straight and went home to his wife, who was rejoicing over the good fortune that had come to them. And of course he didn't speak one word about the Kings's ears to her.

Bifan soon found that the secret was no laughing matter. He itched to tell his friends about it, and it was only the knowledge that King March would certainly cut off his head that restrained him. Keeping the secret got harder and harder as the days went by. It worried Bifan so much that he was afraid he might blurt it out in his sleep and his wife would hear it, and then he was sure to lose his head because his wife would tell everybody. He began to be as sad and unsmiling as King March himself, and got thinner and thinner until at last his wife sent him to see a doctor.

"I have to keep a secret which I daren't tell to anyone else," Bifan blurted out as the doctor started to examine him.

"Ah," said the doctor. "Then I can't cure you. If you don't share your secret with someone else you'll waste away and die. Tell it to someone or something, Bifan. That's my advice. Good day to you."

Bifan went away in despair. then he remembered that the doctor had said '**or something.**' Would that do the trick? Well, he could try! He was passing close to the King's palace just then, and there was a clump of reeds growing under the wall. Bifan put his head in among the reeds and told them his secret, three times.

"March has mule's ears! March has mule's ears! March has mule's ears!"

At once he felt as if a great weight had been lifted from him. He went home smiling once again, and as the days went by he began to grow fatter and fatter.

Some weeks later king March invited the other lords of Wales to a feast in his castle. There were to be harpers and pipers to make music, and from the king of Gwynedd March borrowed the best piper in North Wales, whose name was Enoc. Enoc came walking across the hills to Lleyn with his reed pipe in his wallet, and as he was approaching the castle gate he heard the harps playing and knew he was late. All the same, he took out his reed pipe to make sure it was ready for playing. To his dismay it was broken right across the middle. Then he saw a clump of reeds growing under the castle wall. Lucky for me! thought Enoc, and he cut one of the reeds and made the holes in the right places for the notes before hurrying into the castle.

When he came into the great hall the visiting kings were all sitting at the high table with King March. The harps stopped playing as he entered, and the King saw him.

"Here is Enoc at last," said King March. "Now, Enoc, you shall pipe for us."

Enoc put the reed pipe to his lips and blew. But out of the pipe came words instead of music.

"March has mule's ears! March has mule's ears! March has mule's ears!"

Well, there was a whispering and sniggering then, which King March quelled by springing to his feet. He was pale with anger.

"For this insult, Enoc," he shouted, "I swear I will cut off your head!"

Enoc fell on his knees. "Mercy, lord King!" he cried. "I only blew the notes of a merry tune — the pipe itself turned them into words."

"Bring me that pipe!" thundered March.

Enoc shuffled along the floor on his knees and gave him the pipe. There was a solemn hush in the great hall as the King put it to his lips and blew.

"March has mule's ears! March has mule's ears! March has mule's ears!" came from the pipe.

King March let the reed fall from his fingers. His anger had gone and he looked very sad.

"This reed has learned my secret," he said slowly, "though how, I cannot tell."

Then a little fat man came rushing from the crowd at the other end of the hall and threw himself at the King's feet.

"My lord!" squeaked Bifan the barber. "Forgive me! I told the reeds!" And he stammered out the story of his terrible worry and how it was cured.

When he had ended, King March drew himself to his full height and spoke to everyone there.

"Good people," said he, "I have sworn to cut off the heads of these two men before me. I cannot do this, because what Bifan told the reeds is the truth. I retract my oath. Bifan and Enoc shall go free.

He turned sadly away when he had finished speaking, certain that everyone would laugh and jeer at him now that they knew his secret. A great roar of cheering made him swing round. They were all waving and shouting!

"Long live March the merciful! Long live March the good!"

One voice rose above the rest. "Better mule's ears than cat's claws, lord King!"

And then a new and louder cheering burst forth. King March, for the first time, had been seen to smile.

Glossary

Meaning of Welsh words not otherwise explained in the text.

Bedd — grave.

Bobol anwyl! — Dear People! An expression comparable with the English "Dear me!"

Cader Idris (more correctly Cadair Idris) — Idris's Seat.

Cwm Tregalan — Valley of Death.

Dinas Emrys — Fortress of Ambrosius; Ambrosius — Merlin. The ruins can still be seen near Beddgelert.

Dol-y-Lleian — Meadow of the Nun.

Eryry, the Welsh name for Snowdonia, is sometimes taken to mean "Place of the Eagles," although it is more likely that the Welsh word for "eagle" (eryr) came from Eryri, meaning "Highlands."

Esgob Mawr! — Great Bishop! An exclamation comparable with the English "Good gracious!"

Gwaelod — bottom, in this instance implying "low-lying."

Hafod — Summer Dwelling, as distinct from the sheep farmer's lowland winter home and surrounding pasture.

Llyn — lake.

Llyn-y-dywarchen — Lake of the turf.

Llyn-y-gadair, takes its name from the nearby Mynydd-y-gadair — Mountain of the Chair.

Medrod — Modred in the English stories of King Arthur.

Moel — hill, especially one with a rounded bare top.

Moel Hebog — Hawk's Hill.

Moel-yr-ogof — Hill of the cave.

Noson lawen — Merry evening; a traditional form of Welsh domestic entertainment when a few neighbours gather around the kitchen fire, each contributing a song or a story.

Taid — grandfather.

Also available from
John Jones Publishing Ltd

FEET IN CHAINS by Kate Roberts. Translated from the Welsh by John Idris Jones. "Her characters are motivated by the need to survive poverty with some dignity, independence and self-respect. She is skillful at her craft, welding her short chapters into a strong bridge to link the generations and decades she writes about." *Tribune.* "I urge it strongly for its distillation of time and place and people ... triumphantly alive in their own small corner." *The Guardian.* "A seminal work of Welsh-language fiction and one which has drawn praise from critics, not only in Wales but in England and America. It remains one of the finest novels which I have read by any writer." Dewi Roberts, *Cambrensis* 1996. "It is a mark of the compelling power of this short novel and the vitality of its translation by John Idris Jones that it seems important we should know what Kate Roberts was really saying ... we admire the force of this narrative ..." Richard Jones, *The New Welsh Review,* Autumn 1996.

ISBN 1 871083 80 X   Price: £4.99

TEA IN THE HEATHER by Kate Roberts. Translated by Wyn Griffith. Eight stories set in Caernarfonshire in the early years of the twentieth century. They are clear, historically accurate accounts of the lives of smallholding hill farmers and quarrymen, holding their culture together in the face of deprivation. There is a central link in the presence of the girl Begw; the first story presents her at the age of about three; in the last one she is nine. Her friend Winni is a rebel, old before her time. These are moving, unforgettable stories.

ISBN 1 871083 85 0   Price: £4.99